THE CREEPS 3

CURSE OF THE
ATTACK-O-LANTERNS

Chris Schweizer

AMULET BOOKS
NEW YORK

Library of Congress Control Number: 2016936953

Hardcover ISBN: 978-1-4197-2190-8
Paperback ISBN: 978-1-4197-2191-5

Printed and bound in China
10 9 8 7 6 5 4 3 2 1

Amulet Books are available at special discounts when purchased in quantity for premiums and promotions as well as fundraising or educational use. Special editions can also be created to specification. For details, contact specialsales@abramsbooks.com or the address below.

ABRAMS The Art of Books
115 West 18th Street, New York, NY 10011
abramsbooks.com

SHE SHAN'T MISS **ONE PUMPKIN,** NOT WITH HUNDREDS STILL ON THE VINE.

I DIDN'T MARRY A THIEF.

YOU **MARRIED** A MAN YOU RECKONED WOULD BE A GOOD FATHER.

HOW GOOD A FATHER COULD I BE WERE I TO LET MY GIRLS GO YEAR AFTER YEAR WITHOUT A JACK O' THE LANTERN ON HALLOWS' E'EN?

BETTER THIS PUMPKIN BRING SMILES HERE THAN FLIES IN ITS FIELD.

THE WOMAN'S A WITCH. SHE'LL PUT A HEX ON US IF SHE SUSPECTS.

SHE'S NO MORE WITCH THAN I AM WALRUS. SHE'S JUST A SPITEFUL OLD CRONE WHO WOULD RATHER SEE HER HARVEST ROT THAN LET IT SEED HAPPINESS IN THIS COUNTY.

HERE, NOW. TAKE MISTER O'LANTERN'S INNARDS.

YOU CAN ONE OF YOUR FINE PIES MAKE WHILST I GIVE OUR FRIEND A FACE.

...

THERE!

PAPA, IT'S PERFECT!

NOT YET, IT ISN'T! WHAT USE IS A JACK O' THE LANTERN WITHOUT ITS **CANDLE?**

NOW HE'S PERFECT.

AIEEEE~

MAMA!

WE'VE GOT TO GO BACK FOR MAMA!

NO, SHE TOLD US TO RIDE!

WE CAN'T LEAVE HER, CHARLOTTE!

WE'VE GOT TO!

WE'LL GET HELP!

JUST HOLD ON

6

SWIFTLY!

YOU WRETCHED LITTLE URCHINS!

YOU STOLE ONE OF MY PUMPKINS!

GET BACK HERE!

YOU CAN'T ESCAPE FROM THAT WHICH YOU'VE UNLEASHED!

WE'RE NEARLY TO TOWN!

CHARLOTTE, SOMETHING JUST MOVED BEHIND US!

7

DOWN!

YOU HIDE HERE. I'LL LEAD IT OFF.

WHEN YOU RECKON TIME ENOUGH'S GONE PAST FOR THE WAY TO BE CLEAR, YOU RUN.

YOU.

RUN.

SHE OUGHTN'T HAVE FLED.

I **SAID** THERE COULD BE NO ESCAPE.

I MEAN, YEAH, SHE **WAS** A SPIDER MONSTER, BUT SHE WAS **ALSO** MY FAVORITE TEACHER.

YOUR "FAVORITE TEACHER" WAS PLANNING ON LAYING SPIDER-MONSTER EGGS IN YOUR TORSO THAT WOULD'VE EATEN YOU FROM THE INSIDE OUT!

PRINCIPAL GARISH, CAN I GO NOW?

I NEED TO CHANGE FOR THE FIELD TRIP, AND THESE CREEPS ARE BUMMING ME OUT WITH ALL THEIR WEIRD, GROSS CHEST-EGGS TALK.

GARBY, WE'RE IN THE MIDDLE OF DEFENDING YOU!

I'D RATHER BE PUNISHED FOR TAKING A FEW MARKERS THAN HAVE TO LISTEN TO YOU CREEPS JABBER ON ABOUT **MONSTERS** ALL DAY.

GARBY, YOU MAY GO.

THANKS, PRINCIPAL GARISH!

SO LONG, CREEPS!

WHOA! 'SCUSE ME, SON.

BRENDA, WE HAVE A PROBLEM IN THE GYM.

LOOKS LIKE SOME KIND OF INFESTATION. IF I HAD TO GUESS, I'D RECKON ON JAPANESE SPIDER MONSTERS.

I'M GOING TO NEED SOME HEAVY-DUTY SOLVENTS TO CLEAR THE WEBS OUT OF THERE.

11

MR. PINTO, PLEASE GIVE ME A MOMENT. WE'LL DEAL WITH YOUR JANITORIAL ISSUES JUST AS SOON...

HANG ON...

THE GYM?

IF THERE ARE WEBS IN THE **GYM**, AM I TO ASSUME THAT'S WHERE THIS "BATTLE" OF YOURS WAS FOUGHT?

UM... WELL...

I **KNEW** IT! YOU KIDS WERE TRESPASSING ON SCHOOL GROUNDS AFTER HOURS...

...AGAIN!

PLEASE DON'T SUSPEND US, PRINCIPAL GARISH!

AT LEAST NOT UNTIL AFTER THE FIELD TRIP.

OH, NO, I'M NOT LETTING YOU OFF THAT EASY!

I'M GIVING YOU TROUBLEMAKERS...

...SERVICE DETENTION.

YOU'LL BEGIN YOUR SERVICE DETENTION THIS AFTERNOON.

RUEBEN, PLEASE OPEN THE DETENTION LOG AND MAKE FOUR NEW ENTRIES...

FIRST, **JARVIS CLARK.**

BUT IF I'M NOT HOME TO STIR MY CHLOROMETHANE SOLUTION EVERY SEVENTY MINUTES, IT'LL BECOME TOO VOLATILE FOR THE NEW "CEILING SHOES" GLUE I'VE BEEN WORKING ON!

SECOND, **MITCHELL MAYHEW.**

AW, PRINCIPAL GARISH, NOT THIS WEEKEND! DOCTOR JACKSTRAW IS GOING TO STREAM ENGLISH-DUB BOOTLEGS OF ALL FOUR PSOTNIK MOVIES, AND I **NEED** TO WATCH THEM BECAUSE I KNOW ALMOST **NOTHING** ABOUT UKRAINIAN GOBLIN STORIES!

THIRD, **ROSARIO PLAP.**

-SIGH-

SOMEDAY I'LL BE KNOWN FOR MY IMPECCABLE DESIGN SENSE AND NOT BECAUSE I'M ALWAYS GETTING IN TROUBLE.

AND LASTLY, **CAROL PONDICHERRY.**

IF THIS HURTS MY CHANCES OF BEING ADMITTED INTO THE JUNIOR FORENSICS PROGRAM AT THE CAPITAL THIS SUMMER, THEN I'LL APPEAL ALL THE WAY TO THE SCHOOL BOARD.

JUST GET BACK TO YOUR CLASSROOM BEFORE MS. YAMAMOTO DOES A HEAD COUNT.

I WANT YOU ALL BACK HERE **IMMEDIATELY** AFTER SCHOOL TO BEGIN YOUR PUNISHMENT.

AND KIDS?

"STAY OUT OF TROUBLE WHILE YOU'RE AT THE PUMPKIN PATCH."

I CAN'T **BELIEVE** THAT THE SCHOOL CONSIDERS THIS A WORTHWHILE FIELD TRIP.

WHAT'S WRONG WITH THE PUMPKIN PATCH?

ENTER YE WHO DARE

ARE WE **LEARNING** ANYTHING? IT'S A FUN SEASONAL ACTIVITY, BUT IT'S HARDLY EDUCATIONAL.

IT'S TRADITION!

WE TAKE A SCHOOL TRIP TO THE PATCH **EVERY** YEAR.

IT WOULDN'T FEEL LIKE **FALL** WITHOUT THE PUMPKIN PATCH VISIT.

TRUST ME, CAROL, BY THE TIME WE GET THROUGH ALL OF THE FALL FESTIVAL ACTIVITIES...

...YOU'LL FEEL LIKE YOU GREW UP IN PUMPKINS COUNTY!

ALL RIGHT, KIDS. HERE WE ARE!

IF YOU BROUGHT MONEY TO BUY A PUMPKIN, PICK ONE OUT.

WAIT A SECOND...

WHAT'S **THIS?**

WHAT'S WHAT?

THIS!

THIS ISN'T A PUMPKIN PATCH!

THIS IS JUST A **FIELD** WITH PUMPKINS SPREAD OUT ON IT.

THAT'S WHAT A PUMPKIN PATCH **IS,** CAROL.

NO, A PUMPKIN PATCH IS WHERE PUMPKINS **GROW.**

PUMPKINS GROW ON **VINES.** THERE AREN'T ANY VINES HERE. THE SOIL ISN'T EVEN DISTURBED.

VERY PERCEPTIVE, YOUNG LADY.

THESE PUMPKINS WERE GROWN IN BASKERVILLE AND SHIPPED IN.

WHY?

NOBODY WOULD TRAVEL OUT FOR A DAY OF FUN ON THE FARM AT HARVEST TIME IF WE DIDN'T HAVE **PUMPKINS.**

THIS IS WHAT PEOPLE **COME** FOR!

NO, I MEAN, WHY NOT JUST GROW PUMPKINS?

YOU **CAN'T** GROW PUMPKINS IN PUMPKINS COUNTY.

THEY WON'T TAKE ROOT!

WE DON'T HAVE ANY TROUBLE GROWING OTHER CROPS, EVEN OTHER GOURDS. BUT PUMPKINS?

OUTSIDE OF THE BITTERWOOD PATCH, THERE HASN'T BEEN A PUMPKIN GROWN IN THIS COUNTY IN PROBABLY TWO HUNDRED YEARS!

THAT'S RIDICULOUS! THIS IS **PUMPKINS COUNTY.**

WHY WOULD OUR COUNTY BE NAMED AFTER A VEGETABLE WE CAN'T EVEN GROW?

IT'S **NOT,** MISS PONDICHERRY!

PUMPKINS COUNTY ISN'T NAMED FOR THE **CROP,** BUT FOR ITS **FOUNDER...**

...OBADIAH PUMPKINS.

"OBADIAH PUMPKINS"?

OBADIAH BROUGHT THE FIRST GROUP OF SETTLERS TO THIS REGION MORE THAN TWO HUNDRED YEARS AGO.

YOU KNOW THAT STATUE IN FRONT OF THE COURTHOUSE?

THAT'S OBADIAH!

YOU MEAN THE STATUE OF THE BIG BOOT?

OBADIAH'S BOOT!

"TREAD FORTH FROM WHENCE THOU WOULDST RETURN!"

WE ALL HAD TO MEMORIZE THE FOUNDER SPEECH IN THIRD GRADE.

I WAS SECOND BOOTPRINT IN THE FALL FESTIVAL FOUNDER PLAY.

THIS TOWN IS SO WEIRD.

I'VE GOT BIG PLANS FOR ALL THE PUMPKIN GOOP THAT'S GOING TO BE SCOOPED OUT DURING THE CARVING CONTEST TOMORROW.

I'M GOING TO GATHER IT UP AND DO CHEMISTRY EXPERIMENTS WITH IT.

WHAT ARE YOU YOU EXPECTING WILL HAPPEN, JARVIS?

I'VE GOT NO IDEA.

MAYBE PUMPKIN SEEDS HAVE ENOUGH AMINO ACID TO CREATE A VIOLENT REACTION WHEN MIXED WITH A BICARBONATE.

PUMPKIN SEED **PROJECTILES!**

OR MAYBE PUMPKIN JUICE CONDUCTS ELECTRICITY.

OR MAYBE, AS AN ORGANIC PASTE, IT MIGHT WORK AS A FILLER INGREDIENT IN MY "CEILING SHOES" GLUE!

OR MAYBE PUMPKINS AREN'T GOOD FOR ANYTHING BUT PUMPKIN THINGS LIKE MAKING JACK-O'-LANTERNS OR PUMPKIN PIE.

IF YOU PUT LIMITATIONS ON SOMETHING, YOU'LL NEVER KNOW IF IT CAN EXCEED THEM!

AND EVEN IF I CAN'T FIND A GOOD USE FOR THE GOOP, IT'LL STILL BE A WORTHWHILE UNDERTAKING!

HOW'S THAT?

I COULD GET A WORLD RECORD FOR THE MOST PUMPKIN GOOP STUFFED INTO A KID'S BEDROOM!

I'M SURE YOUR DAD WILL **LOVE** THAT.

YOU **MAY** NOT HAVE ENOUGH **ENERGY** TO DO EXPERIMENTS TOMORROW, JARVIS...

"...IF I KNOW PRINCIPAL GARISH, OUR SERVICE DETENTION JOBS ARE **NOT** GOING TO BE EASY."

ALL RIGHT, RULE BREAKERS, LET'S SEE WHAT JOBS WE'VE GOT FOR YOU.

PUMPKINS COUNTY MIDDLE SCHOOL

WE'VE GOT A **LONG** LIST OF COMMUNITY REQUESTS FOR STUDENT HELP.

GOURMET SORBET NEEDS A KID TO SAMPLE THEIR NEW ICE CREAM FLAVORS...

THE ANIMAL SHELTER NEEDS SOMEONE TO PLAY WITH PUPPIES WHEN THEY'RE UNDERSTAFFED...

THE PUBLIC LIBRARY NEEDS SOMEONE TO READ THROUGH A COLLECTION OF DONATED COMIC BOOKS AND MARK WHICH ONES ARE WORTH PUTTING INTO CIRCULATION...

HOLD ON.

YOU'RE TOYING WITH US, AREN'T YOU?

YES. YES, MISS PONDICHERRY, I AM.

THOSE **ARE** LEGITIMATE COMMUNITY REQUESTS, BUT THEY'RE THE SORT THAT I PASS ALONG TO **GOOD** STUDENTS.

GOOD STUDENTS GET SERVICE DETENTION?

NO, **GOOD** STUDENTS **VOLUNTEER** TO HELP FILL COMMUNITY NEEDS. IT'S GOOD FOR THEIR NEIGHBORS **AND** FOR THEIR OWN ACADEMIC RECORDS.

WE HELP OUR COMMUNITY ALL THE TIME!

HOW MANY TIMES HAVE WE SAVED EVERYONE FROM MONSTERS, PRINCIPAL GARISH?

AND HOW MANY TIMES HAVE YOU BROKEN THE RULES DOING SO?

GOOD STUDENTS DON'T BREAK RULES. **RULE BREAKERS** BREAK RULES.

AND THERE'S ONLY ONE JOB ON THIS LIST SUITABLE FOR RULE BREAKERS...

...ASSISTING THE **SHERIFF.**

OH, NO!

PRINCIPAL GARISH, THAT'S A REALLY BAD IDEA.

OLD SHERIFF OBIE HAS IT IN FOR US!

HE'S STILL MAD ABOUT THE THUNDERBIRD AFFAIR.

LIKE IT OR NOT, HELPING OBIE KRAUT WITH HIS SHERIFF DUTIES IS HOW YOU'LL BE SPENDING YOUR SERVICE DETENTION.

NOW GO WAIT OUT FRONT...

"...THE SHERIFF WILL BE BY TO PICK YOU UP ANY MINUTE."

THIS **CAN'T** BE LEGAL.

HEY, AT LEAST **YOU** GET TO SPEND THE WEEKEND DOING SOMETHING THAT GETS YOU EXCITED.

THIS ISN'T EXCITING!

BUT YOU'VE BEEN BUGGING SHERIFF OBIE TO LET YOU SHADOW HIM FOR **MONTHS!**

YEAH, WHEN HE'S **SOLVING CRIMES.**

BUT PROPERTY SEIZURE? YUCK.

PROPERTY SEIZURE IS AN UNPLEASANT BUT NECESSARY DUTY OF THE SHERIFF'S DEPARTMENT.

LAW ENFORCEMENT **ISN'T** JUST CRACKING CASES AND STOPPING BAD GUYS...

...AND WISHING IT WERE DOESN'T DO ANYBODY ANY GOOD.

NO HUNTING FISHING DRAGING

NO SOLICITING

GO AWAY

PUMPKINS CO SHERIFFS DEPT

NO TRESPASSING

KEEP OUT

YOU AND I BOTH KNOW THAT THIS WHOLE CROP WOULD JUST GO TO SPOIL LIKE IT DOES EVERY YEAR.

AT LEAST **THIS** WAY YOU GET TO KEEP YOUR HOUSE.

SLAM

OBIE...

SHERIFF...

DON'T DO THIS.

GO INSIDE, SAMANTHA.

AT LEAST WAIT UNTIL AFTER HALLOWEEN, SHERIFF. **THEN** YOU CAN TAKE—

GO INSIDE, SAMANTHA.

I'M WARNING YOU, SHERIFF—

NO, I'M WARNING **YOU.** ONE MORE WORD AND I'LL ARREST YOU.

GO.

INSIDE.

FINE.

BUT YOU MARK MY WORDS, OBIE KRAUT...

...YOU'RE GOING TO REGRET THIS.

THE WHOLE **COUNTY** IS GOING TO REGRET THIS.

OO

SLAM

-SIGH-

OKAY, KIDS. TIME TO GET TO WORK.

MITCHELL, UNCLIP THAT BLUE BAG FROM THE TRUCK BED. IT'S GOT THE SHEARS WE'LL BE USING.

USING FOR WHAT?

NO TRESPASSING

KEEP OUT

CAROL...

...I THINK WE'LL BE USING THEM ON **THESE.**

BUT THAT FARMER SAID PUMPKINS DON'T GROW IN PUMPKINS COUNTY!

WHAT HE **SAID** WAS THAT NOBODY'S BEEN ABLE TO GROW PUMPKINS "OUTSIDE OF THE BITTERWOOD PATCH."

THIS MUST BE THE BITTERWOOD PATCH.

BITTERWOOD?!

IS THIS... IS THIS THE **OLD BITTERWOOD FARM?**

YEP.

YA-HOO!

THIS PLACE HAS BEEN NEAR THE TOP OF MY PUMPKINS COUNTY LANDMARK TOUR EVER SINCE I FIRST READ ABOUT IT!

THIS PLACE? IT'S JUST AN OLD HOUSE AND A WALLED-UP GARDEN.

MAYBE **NOW,** BUT GENERATIONS AGO THIS WAS SAID TO BE THE HOME OF A TERRIBLE AND POWERFUL **WITCH!**

GENERATIONS AGO? HECK, IT STILL **IS.**

EVERYBODY KNOWS THAT IF YOU SNEAK INTO OLD LADY BITTERWOOD'S GARDEN, SHE'LL TURN YOU INTO A **TOAD.**

STOW THAT TALK, JARVIS.

THE AMOUNT Y'ALL GET PICKED ON, I'D HAVE FIGURED YOU'D HAVE LEARNED HOW **ROTTEN** IT FEELS TO HAVE FOLKS SPREADING STORIES ABOUT YOU.

YOU THINK IT MAKES HER **HAPPY,** KIDS WHISPERING WHENEVER SHE COMES INTO TOWN?

YOU THINK SHE DOESN'T GET **TERRIFIED** WHENEVER SOME TEENAGER TAKES A DARE TO SNEAK INTO HER YARD?

CALL A LADY A **WITCH,** AND SUDDENLY IT FEELS **OKAY** TO THROW A ROCK THROUGH HER WINDOW OR WRITE CRUEL NOTES ON HER FENCE.

THE AMOUNT OF TIMES I'VE HAD TO SEND A DEPUTY OUT HERE TO...

...

I DON'T WANT TO HEAR ANOTHER MENTION OF WITCHES, **OR** OF SAMANTHA BITTERWOOD.

THAT KIND OF TALK CAUSES MORE HURT THAN YOU'D GUESS.

SORRY, SHERIFF OBIE. I JUST GET EXCITED BY SPOOKY STORIES. I WASN'T THINKING ABOUT HOW THIS ONE MIGHT AFFECT SOMEONE.

YEAH, ME NEITHER. I DON'T WANT TO MAKE OLD LADY BITTERWOOD FEEL BAD OR NOTHIN'.

I KNOW YOU DIDN'T MEAN ANYTHING BY IT. JUST WANT YOU THINKING ABOUT WHAT YOU'RE SAYING, IS ALL.

ALL RIGHT NOW. POP THOSE SHEARS OUT. I WANT YOU KIDS TO SNIP THE VINES ABOUT SIX INCHES OFF THE PUMPKIN.

ONCE YOU'VE CUT THE VINE, CARRY THE PUMPKIN CAREFULLY AND PUT IT IN THE BACK OF THE TRUCK.

OOF!

THESE ARE HEAVIER THAN THEY LOOK.

WHEN THE TRUCK'S FULL, I'LL RUN THEM TO THE STATION, AND YOU CAN START ON THE SECOND LOAD.

SECOND LOAD?

YEP. THE TRUCK CAN PROBABLY HOLD ABOUT THIRTY, MAYBE FORTY, PUMPKINS PER LOAD...

...AND THIS COURT ORDER IS FOR **FIVE HUNDRED** PUMPKINS.

SO LET'S PICK UP THE PACE, KIDS...

"...IT'S GOING TO BE A LONG AFTERNOON."

I THINK MY ARMS ARE GOING TO FALL OFF.

YOUR ARMS CAN'T HURT AS BAD AS MY LEGS. THEY FEEL LIKE WIGGLY OLD NOODLES.

I JUST WANT TO CURL UP IN A BALL AND CRY.

TIRED, TIRED, TIRED — THAT'S US, ALL RIGHT.

WELL, THIS IS THE LAST LOAD, SO SAVE YOUR WHINING UNTIL WE'RE DONE.

WELL, WELL, WELL...

PUMPKINS COUNTY COURT

SHERIFF DEP...

FALL FESTIVAL
SATURDAY
CARVING CONTEST 8AM

...IF IT ISN'T THE **CREEPS.**

THE SHERIFF'S HAD YOU HARD AT WORK, I SEE.

THESE KIDS WORKED REAL HARD, FINN. CUT AND CARRIED A WHOLE LOT OF PUMPKINS.

AND WOULD YOU BELIEVE IT? NOT ONE OF THESE KIDS ENDED UP AT THE SHERIFF'S STATION TODAY!

MAYBE WE SHOULD PUT YOU TROUBLE-MAKERS TO WORK **EVERY** AFTERNOON.

IT'S GETTING PRETTY DARK. I RECKON YOU KIDS BETTER START MAKING FOR HOME.

BUT BEFORE YOU GO...

...GO AHEAD AND GRAB YOURSELF A **PRACTICE PUMPKIN.**

29

WHAT'S A "PRACTICE PUMPKIN"?

FOR THE CONTEST!

THANKS, SHERIFF!

THE HIGHLIGHT OF THE FALL FESTIVAL IS THE JACK-O'-LANTERN CONTEST. BUT YOU CAN'T CARVE THEM AHEAD OF TIME.

EVERYONE CARVES HIS OR HER PUMPKIN TOGETHER, IN FRONT OF THE COURTHOUSE. IT'S A PUMPKINS COUNTY TRADITION!

THAT STILL DOESN'T EXPLAIN WHAT A PRACTICE PUMPKIN IS.

OH! IT'S A PUMPKIN YOU USE FOR WARM-UP. GET USED TO THE TOOLS, MAYBE WORK OUT YOUR COMPOSITION...

GIL HERRINGBONE'S DAD HAS WON THE CONTEST THREE OUT OF THE LAST FIVE YEARS, AND I HEARD THAT **HE** GOES THROUGH LIKE **TWO DOZEN** PRACTICE PUMPKINS.

WOULDN'T IT BE BETTER FOR PEOPLE TO DO THEIR PUMPKINS ON THEIR OWN AND BRING THEM TO THE CONTEST?

THE SETTLERS OF PUMPKINS COUNTY WERE A HARDY BREED, CAROL. THEY WERE TRAPPERS, FARMERS, KEELBOATERS, AND CATTLE DRIVERS.

WHAT DOES THAT HAVE TO DO WITH A PUMPKIN-CARVING CONTEST?

BEING ABLE TO TACKLE A TASK QUICKLY AND UNDER PRESSURE WAS JUST AS IMPORTANT AS BEING ABLE TO DO THAT TASK WELL.

THE SETTLERS NEVER KNEW WHEN A TORNADO OR A BANDIT RAID OR A LOCUST SWARM OR A BEAR ATTACK MIGHT CUT SHORT WHATEVER THEY WERE DOING, AND SO THEY LEARNED TO DO EVERYTHING SWIFTLY AND EFFICIENTLY... PUMPKIN CARVING INCLUDED!

CLARK RESIDENCE. THIS IS JARVIS, MAN OF ACTION.

HEY, JARVIS. ARE YOU BUSY?

BECAUSE I'M HAVING SOME TROUBLE WITH MY PUMPKIN.

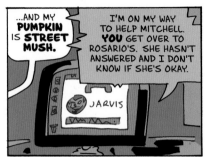

...AND MY **PUMPKIN** IS **STREET MUSH.**

JARVIS

I'M ON MY WAY TO HELP MITCHELL. **YOU** GET OVER TO ROSARIO'S. SHE HASN'T ANSWERED AND I DON'T KNOW IF SHE'S OKAY.

ON IT!

CRIME LAB

ROSARIO!

ARE YOU OKAY?

I SMOOSHED MY PRACTICE PUMPKIN.

IT **WAS** A LOVELY PUMPKIN BEFORE I GOT MY HANDS ON IT.

COME ON!

WHERE ARE WE GOING?

MITCHELL'S HOUSE. HIS PUMPKIN CAME ALIVE AND IS TRYING TO EAT HIM, TOO, JUST LIKE OURS DID.

I'M GLAD TO HEAR IT.

YOU'RE GLAD? HE MIGHT BE IN TERRIBLE DANGER!

WELL, I DON'T WANT HIM TO BE IN TERRIBLE DANGER, BUT IT'S NICE TO KNOW THAT I'M NOT THE **ONLY** ONE WHOSE PUMPKIN CAME TO LIFE.

THAT WOULD HAVE BEEN EMBARRASSING!

IT'S FOR THE BEST, I GUESS. I PROBABLY WOULD HAVE SMASHED MINE ANYWAY.

YOU WOULD HAVE SMASHED IT ANYWAY?

WHY?

ONE OF THE EYES I CARVED WAS JUST A LITTLE BIT CROOKED.

WHAT CAN I SAY? I'M A PERFECTIONIST!

MITCHELL!

HEY, FRIENDS! GOOD TO SEE YOU!

ARE YOU GUYS ALL RIGHT? WHERE'S THE PUMPKIN?

UNDER THE TRASH CAN.

WE SQUISHED IT WITH A CINDER BLOCK AND PUT THIS BIN ON TOP OF IT, JUST TO BE ON THE SAFE SIDE.

I'M SURE GLAD I DIDN'T LIGHT **MINE.** MITCHELL'S NEARLY ATE MY FEET!

WELL, IT **DIDN'T** EAT THEM, AND NOW **WE** HAVE THE REMAINS OF A CARNIVOROUS PUMPKIN TO STUDY FOR OUR CREATURE COMPENDIUM!

EVER HEAR OF ANYTHING LIKE THIS BEFORE, MITCHELL?

NOTHING HELPFUL.

COULD THEY BE ALIENS DISGUISED AS PUMPKINS?

WE CUT THEM RIGHT OFF THE VINE. I THINK THEY'RE REAL PUMPKINS.

WHAT ABOUT A **GHOST?** LIKE, A SOUL THAT WAS TRAPPED IN A PUMPKIN PRISON AND SET FREE WHEN YOU CARVED IT?

IT WOULD HAVE TO BE A PRETTY NEW GHOST. THOSE PUMPKINS ARE ONLY A FEW MONTHS OLD.

MAYBE THE PUMPKINS HAVE BEEN INFESTED WITH A KILLER PARASITE. OR SOME KIND OF SUPER VIRUS!

EVERYBODY TALKS ABOUT THE WEIRD EXPERIMENTS THAT THEY DO UP AT MANITOU LABS. MAYBE THEY WERE WORKING ON A GERM OR A BIOWEAPON OR SOMETHING, AND IT GOT LOOSE!

I THINK WE OUGHT TO WARN SHERIFF OBIE.

BUT WE DON'T KNOW WHAT THESE THINGS ARE YET!

WE DON'T HAVE TO KNOW. **HE'S** THE **SHERIFF.** IT'S **HIS** JOB TO KEEP PEOPLE SAFE AND SOLVE MYSTERIES.

WOULDN'T IT BE NICE IF JUST ONCE WE COULD STAY OUT OF TROUBLE AND LET AN ADULT DEAL WITH THE DANGEROUS MONSTER PROBLEMS?

YOU KIDS OUGHT TO BE ASHAMED OF YOURSELVES.

WHAT? WHY?

I TOLD YOU EARLIER THAT I DIDN'T WANT YOU SPREADING RUMORS ABOUT MS. BITTERWOOD BEING A WITCH, AND WHAT DO YOU DO?

THEY COME HERE WITH SOME CRAZY STORY ABOUT HER ENCHANTED PUMPKINS.

40

HEY, WE ONLY REPORTED A DANGEROUS MONSTER PROBLEM.

WE NEVER SAID **ANYTHING** ABOUT OLD LADY BITTERWOOD BEING INVOLVED.

YEAH, BUT MAYBE WE SHOULD HAVE!

SHE DID SAY THAT THE WHOLE COUNTY WOULD REGRET TAKING HER PUMPKINS...

IF SHE **IS** A WITCH, MAYBE SHE PUT A SPELL ON—

THAT IS **ENOUGH!**

SAMANTHA BITTERWOOD IS JUST A LONELY WOMAN WHO WANTS TO BE LEFT IN PEACE.

SHE'S ALREADY HAD A DIFFICULT DAY, AND THE LAST THING SHE NEEDS IS TO BE DRAGGED INTO ONE OF YOUR RIDICULOUS MONSTER INVESTIGATIONS.

I SAY WE LOCK THEM UP, SHERIFF. YOU **KNOW** THAT THEY'RE GOING TO GET INTO TROUBLE WITH THIS PUMPKIN NONSENSE.

IT'S NOT NONSENSE! WE SAW THEM WITH OUR OWN EYES AND SMASHED THEM WITH OUR OWN STUFF!

SHERIFF OBIE, THE THREE PUMPKINS THAT CAME TO LIFE ALL CAME FROM THE BITTERWOOD PATCH. IF THE REST OF THOSE PUMPKINS DO THE SAME, THEN THE TOWN WILL BE OVERRUN!

YOU NEED TO DESTROY THOSE PUMPKINS!

I'M NOT DESTROYING FIVE HUNDRED PERFECTLY GOOD PUMPKINS BECAUSE YOU THINK IT'S FUNNY TO CONCOCT WILD STORIES THAT CAST ASPERSIONS ON A POOR OLD LADY.

THOSE PUMPKINS WILL BE PROVIDED TO ANYONE WHO WANTS TO ENTER THE CARVING CONTEST AT TOMORROW'S FALL FESTIVAL, NOT SMASHED FOR YOUR WEIRD AMUSEMENT.

NOW GET HOME.

AND WHEN I SAY HOME, I MEAN **HOME.**

IF I CATCH YOU KIDS OUT TONIGHT...

...OR IF I HEAR THAT YOU'VE BOTHERED MS. BITTERWOOD...

...YOU'RE **TOAST.**

FINN, YOU WERE GOING TO CARVE A COUPLE OF PUMPKINS FOR THE STEPS, WEREN'T YOU?

PLANNING ON IT.

I'M NOT PUTTING ANY STOCK IN THAT FOOL TALE THOSE KIDS WERE SPINNING, BUT EVEN SO...

...IF ANYTHING SEEMS UNUSUAL WHEN YOU CARVE THEM, GIVE ME A CALL, OKAY?

YOU GOT IT, SHERIFF.

I'LL SEE YOU GUYS TOMORROW.

ROSARIO, WHAT ARE YOU DOING?

THIS IS THE FASTEST WAY HOME FOR ME.

WE'RE NOT GOING HOME.

BUT SHERIFF OBIE SAID—

WE'RE GOING TO OLD LADY BITTERWOOD'S PUMPKIN PATCH TO SEE IF WE CAN FIND CLUES.

BUT SHERIFF OBIE SAID—

ROSARIO, IF WE DON'T DO SOMETHING ABOUT THESE PUMPKINS, THEN A LOT OF PEOPLE MIGHT GET HURT.

BUT SHERIFF OBIE SAID—

AND IF YOU DON'T HELP US, **WE** MIGHT GET HURT WHILE TRYING TO SAVE THE TOWN.

...

-SIGH-

THAT'S HER SIGH OF RESIGNED AGREEMENT!

LET'S GO!

CLICK

COME ON!

COME ON WHERE?

TO SPY ON OLD LADY BITTERWOOD, OF COURSE!

WE'RE LOOKING FOR CLUES, NOT SPYING ON OLD LADIES!

SPYING **IS** LOOKING FOR CLUES.

YOU SHOULDN'T SPY ON LADIES!

WHAT IF SHE'S IN HER **UNDERWEAR?!**

I'M A MAN OF ACTION, ROSARIO. IF I HAVE TO SEE AN OLD LADY'S UNDERWEAR TO SAVE THE COUNTY, THEN BY GUM I'LL—

IF THERE'S SPYING TO BE DONE, JARVIS, IT PROBABLY OUGHT TO BE DONE BY ME.

WHY? I'M A GREAT SPY!

YOU'RE GREAT AT GETTING INTO PLACES THAT OTHER PEOPLE CAN'T, BUT CAROL IS BETTER AT NOTICING THINGS THAT OTHER PEOPLE MISS.

I GUESS THAT'S TRUE.

IF **I** WERE AN OLD LADY AND WAS BEING SPIED ON, I'D RATHER BE SPIED ON BY ANOTHER LADY THAN BY A BOY IN CAMOUFLAGE PANTS.

MOST LADIES WOULD RATHER NOT BE SPIED ON AT ALL.

WE'RE JUST BEING THOROUGH, ROSARIO. IF OLD LADY BITTERWOOD **DOES** HAVE SOMETHING TO DO WITH THE PUMPKINS COMING TO LIFE, THEN IT'S **OUR** DUTY TO FIND OUT SO WE CAN STOP HER.

HRMPH.

WAIT, WHAT'S THAT?

WHAT'S **WHAT?**

THERE, ON THE GROUND! THAT GLINT OF WHITE.

IS IT A CLUE? IF IT'S A CLUE, THEN WE DON'T HAVE TO SPY ON OLD LADIES IN THEIR UNDERWEAR!

IT MIGHT BE A CLUE.

IT'S A **SKULL!**

EWWW!

A SKULL?

LIKE, A **REAL** SKULL?

≷GASP!≷

IT LOOKS LIKE IT.

OLD LADY BITTERWOOD'S PUMPKIN PATCH IS A **SECRET CEMETERY!**

THE PUMPKINS ARE POSSESSED BY THE SOULS OF HER **MURDERED VICTIMS!**

YOU THINK OLD LADY BITTERWOOD **MURDERED** THIS POOR LITTLE **SQUIRREL**?

THAT MONSTER!

DADGUMMIT, MITCHELL, YOU CAN'T SAY "IT'S A SKULL" AND EXPECT PEOPLE TO KNOW YOU'RE TALKING ABOUT AN **ANIMAL** SKULL!

WE FIGURED YOU WERE TALKING ABOUT **PEOPLE** SKULLS.

HEY, A SQUIRREL IS A LIVING BEING, TOO. SHOW SOME COMPASSION, HUH?

I DON'T THINK THAT THE PUMPKINS ARE POSSESSED BY THE GHOSTS OF **MURDERED SQUIRRELS.**

THEY MIGHT BE! THERE'S PLENTY OF PRECEDENT FOR ANIMAL GHOSTS IN FOLKLORE FROM ALL OVER THE WORLD.

YEAH, BUT THEY'RE PROBABLY **COOL** ANIMALS, LIKE WOLVES OR VULTURES OR TIGER SHARKS.

SQUIRRELS **ARE** COOL!

HEY, GUYS, THERE'S SOMETHING YOU NEED TO SEE BACK HERE.

IT'S THE BODIES OF HUNDREDS OF MURDERED SQUIRRELS, ISN'T IT?

SHHH!

BLESS THIS HOME

I KNEW IT! SHE'S A WITCH! LOOK, SHE'S GOT A CAULDRON.

THAT'S NOT A CAULDRON—IT'S A CROCK-POT.

SHE **WAS** TALKING TO HER CAT EARLIER.

WITCHES **ARE** SAID TO EMPLOY ANIMALS AS "FAMILIARS"... ENVOYS BETWEEN THEMSELVES AND THE SPIRIT REALM.

MY AUNT DELFINA TALKS TO **HER** CAT. THAT DOESN'T MAKE **HER** A WITCH.

THAT COULD BE A BOOK OF SPELLS. IT LOOKS OLD.

OR IT **COULD** BE A **RECIPE BOOK.** REMEMBER WHAT SHERIFF OBIE SAID ABOUT HOW HURTFUL THESE WITCH RUMORS ARE.

IF WE COULD SEE WHAT INGREDIENTS SHE'S USING, MAYBE THAT WOULD GIVE US A HINT AS TO WHAT SHE'S UP TO.

I'VE GOT AN IDEA!

48

WE CAN'T SEE THAT FAR, BUT I CAN USE MY **PHONE CAMERA** AND ZOOM IN REALLY CLOSE.

BLESS THIS HOME

YOU FORGOT TO TURN YOUR FLASH OFF.

MAYBE SHE DIDN'T NOTICE.

49

AAAAAUGH!

RUN!

OKAY, WE'RE PRETTY DARN DEEP IN THE WOODS NOW. I THINK WE'RE GOOD.

DO YOU THINK SHE SAW US?

OF COURSE SHE SAW US! YOUR FLASH WENT OFF!

WELL, LET'S TAKE A LOOK AND SEE WHETHER THE PICTURE GAVE US A CLUE.

WE'LL JUST ZOOM IN ON THE ZOOM-IN...

WHAT DOES IT SAY?

IT SAYS "EYE OF NEWT"! SHE'S A WITCH, FOR SURE.

WE CAN'T SEE THE WHOLE THING. IT MIGHT JUST AS EASILY SAY "EYE ON NEW JERSEY."

ROSARIO, A WITCH WOULDN'T PUT "EYE ON NEW JERSEY" IN A MAGIC POTION. THAT'S JUST SILLY.

MAYBE IT'S A BRAND NAME. "EYE ON NEW JERSEY" BRAND PAPRIKA OR SOMETHING.

PAPRIKA'S RED. I VOTE WITCH. **EYE OF NEWT,** ROSARIO!

IT'S THE MOST WITCHY INGREDIENT THERE IS!

IT'S **HILARIOUSLY** WITCHY! LIKE IF YOU WERE A CARTOON WITCH, YOU'D SAY "WHERE'S THAT EYE OF NEWT?"

IT COULD BE YOUR FUNNY CATCH PHRASE!

THAT'S NOT A VERY FUNNY CATCH PHRASE.

WELL, MAYBE THAT'S WHY CARTOON WITCHES AREN'T ESPECIALLY POPULAR.

IF IT **IS** EYE OF NEWT SHE'S MIXING INTO THAT CAULDRON, THEN THAT'S OUR EVIDENCE.

EVIDENCE OF WHAT?

I DON'T KNOW. STEREOTYPICAL WITCHINESS.

WE NEED **SOMETHING** TO CONVINCE SHERIFF OBIE THAT THE PUMPKINS ARE DANGEROUS!

HOW DANGEROUS CAN THEY BE? WE SQUISHED OURS EASY.

YOU JUST THINK THAT BECAUSE YOU'RE SO TOUGH. MITCHELL AND ME BARELY MADE IT!

THE FOUR OF US HAVE PRACTICE DODGING MONSTERS, BUT REGULAR PEOPLE?

THEY MIGHT NOT BE AS QUICK ON THEIR FEET AS US. I DON'T KNOW WHAT HAPPENS IF A PUMPKIN GETS YOU, BUT I DON'T WANT TO FIND OUT AT SOME DUMB OLD HARVEST FESTIVAL WITH HUNDREDS OF THEM COMING TO LIFE AT ONCE.

THE HARVEST FESTIVAL **ISN'T** DUMB, CAROL.

YEAH, IT'S PRETTY GREAT. YAM-CANDIED CODFISH, CORN CIDER, DUNK THE OCTOGENARIAN...

YOU'LL SEE. THE PUMPKINS COUNTY HARVEST FESTIVAL IS THE BEST EVENT OF THE YEAR.

IT'LL BE THE MOST **DISASTROUS** EVENT OF THE YEAR UNLESS WE GET THE SHERIFF TO DESTROY THOSE PUMPKINS!

OH, YOU **HAVE** HELPED! I'VE BEEN ITCHING TO CHARGE YOU MISCREANTS SINCE YOU FIRST STARTED MAKING TROUBLE...

...AND NOW YOU BRING ME **PROOF** OF YOUR MISDEEDS! I CAN RUN YOU UP FOR TRESPASSING, VOYEURISM, ILLEGAL SURVEILLANCE...

YEAH, BUT YOUR "PROOF" IS EVIDENCE WE'RE **RIGHT** ABOUT THE **PUMPKINS!**

YOU BROUGHT ME A GRAINY PICTURE OF WHAT YOU **SAY** IS MS. BITTERWOOD'S HAND HOLDING A JAR WITH A LABEL THAT I CAN'T READ.

SO FAR AS EVIDENCE GOES, THIS MIGHT BE THE LOUSIEST I'VE EVER SEEN.

I'LL PROCESS YOUR CHARGES SOON, AND THEN I'LL CALL YOUR PARENTS.

YOU'RE NOT PROCESSING THEM NOW?

DON'T GO THINKING THIS IS ONE OF SHERIFF OBIE'S BLUFFS WHERE HE THREATENS YOU, THEN LETS YOU GO WITH A WARNING. YOU **WILL** BE CHARGED...

...**AFTER** I FINISH WITH THESE PUMPKINS.

54

YOU WANT EVIDENCE? **THIS** IS YOUR EVIDENCE.

EVIDENCE THAT YOU CREEPS ARE NOTHING BUT A BUNCH OF LIARS AND MUCKRAKERS!

THREE PUMPKINS FROM THE BITTERWOOD PATCH CARVED INTO JACK-O'-LANTERNS, AND NOT **ONE** OF THEM BROUGHT TO LIFE.

THEY DON'T COME TO LIFE UNTIL YOU PUT A CANDLE INSIDE!

OH!

YOU MEAN LIKE THIS CANDLE HERE?

NO, IT'S...

THE CANDLE HAS TO BE **LIT**, OF COURSE!

OH, OF COURSE!

THE PUMPKINS FROM THE PATCH ARE DANGEROUS. WAIT, THEY AREN'T? OH, YOU HAVE TO **CARVE** THEM. THAT IS TO SAY, YOU HAVE TO PUT A **CANDLE** IN THEM. WAIT, I MEAN YOU HAVE TO **LIGHT** THE CANDLE. OH, I FORGOT, YOU HAVE TO WEAR A BANANA COSTUME AND RECITE THE GETTYSBURG ADDRESS.

ONE...

TWO...

THREE.

THERE. THREE LIT CANDLES, **NO** ATTACK-O-LANTERNS.

AW, MAN!

WHAT'S THE MATTER, MAYHEW? FINALLY RUN OUT OF LIES AND NONSENSE?

NO, I JUST WISH **I** HAD COME UP WITH "ATTACK-O-LANTERNS."

REAL SOLID MONSTER NAME, DEPUTY FINN.

I FIGURED THEY'D BE MOVING BY NOW.

OOH! TRY PUTTING THEIR TOPS ON, DEPUTY FINN.

-SIGH-

YOU KIDS REALLY ARE THE WORST.

CAREFUL, DEPUTY FINN! KEEP YOUR FINGERS AWAY FROM THEIR MOUTHS.

THAT'S **ENOUGH**, MAYHEW!

YOU MIGHT **THINK** YOU'RE FUNNY, BUT, MISTER, YOU **AREN'T.**

YOUR ANTICS AND MISCHIEF PULL OUR ATTENTION AWAY FROM IMPORTANT SHERIFF BUSINESS!

THIS COUNTY HAS **ENOUGH** TROUBLE WITHOUT YOUR LITTLE GANG ALWAYS...

...

DEPUTY FINN?

DEPUTY FINN, ARE YOU OKAY?

MAYBE...

...JUST MAYBE...

WE'VE GOT TO GET OUT AND STOP THEM BEFORE THEY EAT ANYONE ELSE!

JARVIS, CAN YOU PICK THE LOCK?

DEPUTY FINN TOOK MY UTILITY BELT. MY MAIN SET OF PICKS WAS IN THERE.

WHAT ABOUT YOUR BACKUP SET?

I DISGUISED IT AS FANCY JEWELRY FOR CAROL AND ROSARIO.

AND I TOLD YOU WHEN YOU GAVE IT TO ME THAT I DON'T WEAR JEWELRY.

I DO, BUT **THAT** JEWELRY WAS HIDEOUS, SO I THREW IT AWAY.

YOU DIDN'T GIVE **ME** ANY DISGUISED JEWELRY, JARVIS!

I MADE **YOU** THAT PAPIER-MACHE **MOON MENACE** MASK!

WHAT ABOUT YOUR CARGO POCKETS?

WHAT ABOUT THEM?

THEY'RE USUALLY PACKED WITH USEFUL STUFF THAT DOESN'T FIT IN YOUR UTILITY BELT!

USUALLY, YEAH. BUT I FILLED THEM WITH SPIDER-MONSTER WEBS FROM THE GYM.

EW!

WHY WOULD YOU TOUCH THAT GUNK AFTER WE WERE STUCK TO THE WALL WITH IT?

I FIGURED IT MIGHT BE USEFUL MAKING MY CEILING SHOES GLUE.

I HAVEN'T FOUND A COMPOUND YET THAT WILL STICK STRONG ENOUGH TO HOLD ME ON THE CEILING BUT THAT I CAN PULL FREE FROM TO WALK.

OKAY, SO JARVIS DOESN'T HAVE ANY GEAR ON HIM... ANY OTHER IDEAS AS TO HOW WE COULD GET OUT?

WE COULD CALL FOR HELP.

DEPUTY FINN TOOK OUR PHONES.

I MEANT LIKE THIS:

HELLLP!

Z Z Z

Z WHAT IN HOT HAM HEAVEN IS GOING ON HERE?!

WHY ARE YOU KIDS IN THE HOLDING CELL?

WHERE'S MY DEPUTY?

DEPUTY FINN LOCKED US IN HERE.

Z

AND THEN HE... ...UM...

HE GOT EATEN WHOLE BY ATTACK-O-LANTERNS! IT WAS HORRIBLE!

HE ALSO CAME UP WITH THE NAME "ATTACK-O-LANTERN." CREDIT WHERE CREDIT'S DUE.

FINN! GET OUT HERE!

FINN!

WE TOLD YOU, SHERIFF OBIE — HE GOT EATEN!

FINN!

FINN, YOU'D BETTER NOT BE HOLED UP ASLEEP!

SHERIFF!

DEPUTY FINN IS **GONE.** WE **SAW** HIM GET GOBBLED UP BY OLD LADY BITTERWOOD'S PUMPKINS.

FINN? CALL ME BACK AS SOON AS YOU GET THIS.

SOONER THAN THAT, EVEN.

DADGUMMED DEPUTY LOCKS UP MINORS UNSUPERVISED OVERNIGHT AND NOW HE CAN'T BE BOTHERED TO ANSWER HIS DANG PHONE.

SHERIFF, HAVE YOU HEARD A SINGLE WORD I'VE SAID?

I HEARD YA. I JUST AIN'T LISTENING.

SHERIFF OBIE, THE PUMPKINS ARE **EXTREMELY** DANGEROUS!

ENOUGH WITH THIS PUMPKIN PRANK!

IT'S **NOT** FUNNY. I'VE LOST A LOT OF DEPUTIES IN THE LINE OF DUTY, AND YOU MAKING A GAME OUT OF FINN BEING LATE ISN'T A JOKE ANY MORE THAN YOUR CALLING SAMANTHA A WITCH.

OH. ABOUT THAT...

...WEEEEE SNUCK AROUND OLD LADY BITTERWOOD'S HOUSE AND SAW HER MIXING UP A MAGIC POTION.

SLAM!

GUESS I CAN KISS MY CHANCES OF GETTING HIM TO WRITE ME A LETTER OF RECOMMENDATION FOR JUNIOR FORENSICS GOODBYE.

AT LEAST I GOT MY BELT BACK.

SO WHAT NOW?

WE TRY AND FIGURE OUT HOW TO STOP THE FALL FESTIVAL CARVING CONTEST, I GUESS.

STOP THE CONTEST?!

COULDN'T WE JUST GET THEM TO USE SAFER PUMPKINS?

JEEZ, WHAT IS IT WITH YOU GUYS AND THIS FESTIVAL?

IT'S THE BEST TIME OF THE YEAR, CAROL!

THE LEAVES ARE CHANGING, THE AIR IS CRISP, AND EVERYONE IN TOWN PARTICIPATES IN SOMETHING THAT'S FUN AND SPOOKY!

PLUS YOUR PUMPKIN SAYS A LOT ABOUT WHAT KIND OF PERSON YOU ARE.

YEAH, PEOPLE WHO MIGHT MAKE SNAP JUDGMENTS ABOUT YOU BECAUSE OF HOW YOU LOOK OR WHAT YOU LIKE

(OR THE NUMBER OF TIMES YOU'VE BEEN INVOLVED IN BIG DISASTERS)

WILL TAKE THE TIME TO REALLY LOOK AT YOUR JACK-O'-LANTERN. THEY'LL KNOW YOU BETTER, JUST LIKE YOU'LL KNOW THEM BETTER.

THE WARM FUZZIES YOU GET FROM COMMUNAL VEGETABLE CRAFTING AREN'T WORTH PEOPLE **GETTING EATEN ALIVE!**

HEY!

YOUR FRIEND IS A HEAVY SLEEPER.

-SNORT-

FIVE MORE MINUTES AUNT DELPHINA

zzZ

YOU KIDS HAVE NO IDEA HOW LUCKY YOU ARE RIGHT NOW.

IF I WEREN'T SADDLED WITH THE FESTIVAL AND TRYING TO FIND MY DEPUTY, YOU'D BE IN A WORLD OF TROUBLE.

HECK, YOU **ARE** IN A WORLD OF TROUBLE. I'M GOING TO HAVE PRINCIPAL GARISH EXTEND YOUR SERVICE DETENTION INDEFINITELY.

NOW GET DOWN TO THE SQUARE AND GET WORKING. THERE'S A LOT OF PUMPKIN GOOP TO GATHER UP TODAY, AND I WANT YOU TAKING CARE OF IT **FIRST THING,** YOU GOT ME?

AWW, SHERIFF OBIE, YOU CAN'T MAKE US WORK DURING THE CONTEST!

MITCHELL, THE CONTEST IS THE LOWEST PRIORITY RIGHT NOW!

I'M DOING ALL THAT I CAN TO KEEP YOU STINKERS FROM PERMANENTLY RUINING YOUR LIVES.

I DON'T WANT TO PUT YOU IN THE SYSTEM. I DON'T WANT TO SEND YOU OFF TO A JUVENILE DETENTION CENTER. I DON'T WANT YOU YANKED OUT OF SCHOOL OR TAKEN FROM YOUR FAMILIES.

I GIVE YOU CHANCE AFTER CHANCE AFTER CHANCE TO SHAPE UP, AND YOU JUST KEEP PULLING THESE STUNTS.

NO MORE CHANCES. YOU TOW THE LINE FROM HERE ON OUT OR I'LL TREAT YOU LIKE I WOULD ANY OTHER LAWBREAKER, KIDS OR NOT.

NOW **GET.**

I KNEW WE BUGGED HIM, BUT I DIDN'T THINK SHERIFF OBIE **HATED** US.

HE DOESN'T HATE US. HE WOULDN'T TRY TO KEEP US OUT OF TROUBLE IF HE HATED US.

HE HATES US.

SO HERE'S WHAT I'M THINKING: ALL OF THE PUMPKINS WERE PILED TOGETHER IN THE PARKING DECK OF THE COURTHOUSE.

WE GET INTO A MAINTENANCE CLOSET, AND JARVIS CAN PICK OUT SOMETHING **REALLY** FLAMMABLE...

CAROL!

WERE YOU NOT WITH US WHEN SHERIFF OBIE JUST READ US THE RIOT ACT?

LET'S JUST DO WHAT WE'RE SUPPOSED TO. IF THINGS GO BAD, THEN **HE** CAN HANDLE IT.

PLEASE. I DON'T LIKE GETTING IN TROUBLE AT ALL. I CAN'T BEAR TO THINK ABOUT GETTING IN SO MUCH THAT I'D GET SENT OFF TO KID JAIL.

SPIT ON THAT JAZZ!

HUH?

IF WE GET IN TROUBLE, THEN WE GET IN TROUBLE.

IF WE DON'T DO EVERYTHING WE CAN TO TRY AND STOP SOMETHING TERRIBLE FROM HAPPENING, THEN WE MIGHT AS WELL BE DOING THE TERRIBLE THING WITH OUR OWN HANDS.

YOU GUYS DON'T HAVE TO HELP ME, BUT YOU'D BETTER NOT AIM TO CONVINCE ME TO HOLD OFF WHEN I'M **TRYING** TO DO WHAT I KNOW IS THE RIGHT THING.

YOU CAN SCRAM IF YOU WANT.

SPIT ON **THAT** JAZZ!

UH-OH.

GUESS OUR GET-ALL-THE-PUMPKINS-IN-ONE-FELL-SWOOP PLAN DOESN'T WORK IF THEY'VE ALREADY BEEN HANDED OUT.

THERE'S MY SIS AND LITTLE BRO...

HEY!

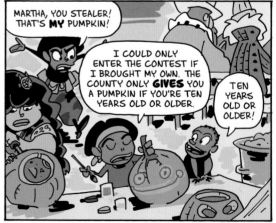

MARTHA, YOU STEALER! THAT'S **MY** PUMPKIN!

I COULD ONLY ENTER THE CONTEST IF I BROUGHT MY OWN. THE COUNTY ONLY **GIVES** YOU A PUMPKIN IF YOU'RE TEN YEARS OLD OR OLDER.

TEN YEARS OLD OR OLDER!

YOU'RE NOT EVEN **CARVING** IT. YOU'RE JUST PAINTING IT!

THAT PUMPKIN'S SPECIAL, MARTHA. IT'S GOT FLASH, AND IT'S **MINE.** I ALREADY STARTED WORKING ON IT!

WELL I GUESS YOU SHOULDN'T HAVE STAYED OUT ALL NIGHT.

WHAT DOES THAT HAVE TO DO WITH ANYTHING?

DAD SAID I COULD HAVE THE PUMPKIN, PROBABLY AS A WAY OF SHOWING YOU JUST HOW HOPPING MAD HE IS THAT YOU DIDN'T COME HOME.

DAD, DAD, HOPPIN' MAD!

HE'LL BE EVEN MADDER IF YOU GET YOUR FACES EATEN OFF, I'D BET!

WHICH IS WHAT'S GOING TO **HAPPEN** IF YOU DON'T GET **OUT** OF HERE. THE PUMPKINS WILL **EAT YOUR FACES OFF.**

WHAAH!

REAL NICE, JARVIS. I'M GOING TO TELL DAD HOW YOU TRIED TO RUIN THE FALL FESTIVAL FOR US BY BEING SCARY.

I'M **TRYING** TO SAVE YOUR FACES FROM GETTING EATEN RIGHT OFF YOUR HEADS, **PUMPKIN STEALER!**

JARVIS, **LOOK!**

71

OLD LADY BITTERWOOD! WHAT'S SHE UP TO?

SOMETHING WITCHY, I' EXPECT. DID YOU SEE THAT CONTRAPTION SHE WAS CARRYING? I'LL BET IT'S FULL OF WITCH'S BREW.

HER PUMPKINS ALREADY COME TO LIFE AND EAT PEOPLE. I DON'T SEE HOW WHATEVER'S IN THAT TANK COULD MAKE THINGS ANY WORSE.

AW, USE YOUR IMAGINATION, ROSARIO!

THAT POTION MIGHT MAKE THE PUMPKINS GROW GIGANTIC, OR GIVE THEM LASER EYES, OR MAKE THEM FLY WITH BIG CREEPY VINE-LEAF WINGS.

LOOK!

WE'VE GOT TO GET UP THERE, FAST!

WHIRRRRRRRRR

WHAT IS THAT THING?

I DON'T KNOW, BUT I WANT ONE!

IT LOOKS LIKE SOMEBODY CROSSED A YARD SPRAYER WITH A LEAF BLOWER.

WHIRRRR VRMMM

OOF!

ALL RIGHT...

...TIME TO SHOW THIS UNGRATEFUL COUNTY WHAT I CAN DO.

SHE'S GOING TO USE THAT THING TO SPRAY THE WHOLE SQUARE!

NOT IF WE STOP HER FIRST!

HOLD IT RIGHT THERE, OLD LADY BITTERWOOD!

I ALREADY KNOW THAT I'M AN OLD LADY. YOU **DON'T** HAVE TO MAKE IT PART OF MY **NAME,** THANKS.

OKAY, HOLD IT RIGHT THERE, MS. BITTERWOOD!

DOCTOR.

HUH?

IT'S **DR.** BITTERWOOD. I HOLD A PHD IN PHYTOCHEMISTRY FROM BASKERVILLE UNIVERSITY.

THAT SOUNDS SCIENCY.

MAYBE SHE'S NOT A WITCH AT ALL.

MAYBE SHE'S A MAD SCIENTIST!

WHATEVER SHE IS, WE'RE GOING TO STOP HER!

GO AWAY, KIDS. I'M BUSY RIGHT NOW AND I **DON'T** NEED **DISTRACTIONS.**

WE'VE BEEN CALLED A LOT OF THINGS, DOC...

SET THIS BABY ON ROCK AND ROLL!

I ASSUME THAT MEANS OPEN THE VALVE ALL THE WAY.

GET AWAY FROM THAT, YOU MEDDLING HOOLIGANS!

DON'T TOUCH THAT TRIGGER!

DO IT, JARVIS!

CLICK

GLUG GLUG GLUG GLUG GLUG

HSSS

IS IT EMPTY?

YOU BET YOUR ELBOWS IT IS!

YEAH!

LOOKS LIKE WE THWARTED YOUR PLAN, DOCTOR BITTERWOOD!

YEAH. YOU DID.

ATTENTION, PUMPKINS COUNTY PUMPKIN CARVERS!

YOUR TIME IS NOW UP!

PLACE YOUR CANDLES IN YOUR JACK-O'-LANTERNS AND MAKE SURE THAT YOUR NAME IS ON THE CARD UNDERNEATH, SO FOLKS KNOW WHO THEY'RE VOTING FOR!

OH, NO!

MAYBE HER SPELL OR FORMULA OR WHATEVER HAS WORN OFF BY NOW AND THAT'S WHY SHE WAS PLANNING ON SPRAYING THE PUMPKINS.

MAYBE WE **ALREADY DID** EVERYTHING WE NEEDED TO DO TO SAVE EVERYONE WHEN WE SPRAYED THAT STUFF DOWN THE DRAIN!

HEY, DOC, HAS WHATEVER MAKES THOSE PUMPKINS COME TO LIFE WORN OFF?

NO.

SIS!

HEY, SIS!

WHAT?

RUN HOME, DOUBLE TIME!

DAD GAVE ME YOUR PUMPKIN, JARVIS! DEAL WITH IT!

JUST LEAVE IT AND RUN HOME AS FAST AS YOU CAN!

NO WAY, JARVIS!

YEAH, NO WAY, JARVIS!

IF YOU GO NOW, YOU CAN MOVE INTO MY ROOM!

PSSH!

I'D RATHER SHARE WITH HARVEY THAN YOU. HE TAKES UP LESS SPACE!

I TAKE UP LESS SPACE!

NO, I MEAN YOU CAN HAVE MY ROOM. I'LL MOVE IN WITH HARVEY!

HE'LL MOVE IN WITH ME!

FOR REAL? YOU THREW A HOT FIT TO GET YOUR OWN ROOM.

FOR REAL, BUT YOU GUYS HAVE TO LEAVE RIGHT NOW.

LIKE, IF I COUNT TO TEN AND YOU'RE STILL IN THE SQUARE, DEAL'S OFF, MARTHA!

COME ON, HARVEY!

COME ON HARVEY!

I'D BETTER NOT SEE YOU SLOW DOWN—

UH-OH.

SAMANTHA...

WHAT HAVE YOU DONE?

WHAT THE HECK DID YOU BUSYBODIES THROW AT MY SHOE?

JAPANESE SPIDER-MONSTER WEBS.

CALL OFF YOUR PUMPKINS, BITTERWOOD.

YOU WANT THESE PUMPKINS TO STOP ATTACKING YOUR NEIGHBORS?

THERE'S JUST **ONE THING** THAT CAN STOP THEM.

IT'S A METHOD THAT I ALONE KNOW HOW TO DO.

IT CAN'T STOP THEM PERMANENTLY, BUT IT'LL GIVE YOU AN HOUR OR SO... TIME ENOUGH TO DESTROY THEM.

BUT I'M NOT SAYING ANOTHER WORD UNTIL MY FOOT IS FREE.

THIS ISN'T BUDGING.

TRY THE LACES.

HECK, **I** COULD'VE JUST TAKEN MY SHOE OFF. NOW WHAT? I'M SUPPOSED TO WALK AROUND WITH ONE SHOE?

THERE! FREE AS A FIDDLER.

NOW YOU TELL US HOW TO STOP THOSE PUMPKINS!

THERE'S A **MAGIC POTION** THAT I KNOW HOW TO BREW.

MAGIC POTION? I KNEW IT! SHE **IS** A WITCH!

SAY SOMETHING ABOUT IT, SKINNY MISTER, AND SEE WHAT HAPPENS.

THIS POTION — HOW LONG DOES IT TAKE TO MAKE?

WE'RE NOT DOING MUCH GOOD HERE ON THE ROOF. LET'S DO THE TALKING WHILE WE'RE WALKING, HUH?

THE POTION DOESN'T TAKE VERY LONG TO MAKE, BUT IT **DOES** REQUIRE SOME INCREDIBLY RARE, TOUGH-TO-FIND INGREDIENTS.

I'VE HAD THE FORESIGHT TO SPEND THE LAST **THIRTY YEARS** COLLECTING THOSE INGREDIENTS. I'M PROUD TO SAY THAT I WAS ABLE TO GET MY HANDS ON ALL OF THEM.

WELL, LET'S GET TO YOUR HOUSE, AND MAKE THAT POTION QUICK!

I ALREADY MADE IT.

DECADES OF HARD-BOUGHT PIECES OF THIS AND THAT, HERBS THAT NO LONGER GROW, ANIMALS THAT NO LONGER LIVE, AND BRIC-A-BRAC FROM EVERY CORNER OF THE GLOBE, ALL MIXED UP INTO THE ONE BREW THAT CAN PUT THE BRAKES ON SUCH A POWERFUL AND ANCIENT CURSE.

IRREPLACEABLE INGREDIENTS, USED TO THE LAST OUNCE IN ONE DESPERATE FINAL ATTEMPT TO STEM THE MURDEROUS TIDE OF THESE DREADED PUMPKINS.

AND **YOU** SPRAYED IT **ALL** DOWN A DRAIN.

SO CONGRATULATIONS, KIDS. YOU'VE DOOMED EVERYONE HERE TO A TERRIBLE END.

THERE'S NOTHING I CAN DO NOW EXCEPT TRY TO GET **OUT** OF THIS COUNTY BEFORE I'M **EATEN ALIVE.**

SO LONG, CHUMPS!

WE'VE DOOMED THE COUNTY.

NOT YET WE HAVEN'T!

BUT DOCTOR BITTERWOOD SAID —

DOCTOR BITTERWOOD'S POTION MIGHT HAVE BEEN THE ONLY WAY TO STOP THEM ALL AT ONCE, BUT WE CAN STILL TAKE THEM OUT ONE BY ONE.

THEY'RE JUST HOLLOWED-OUT PUMPKINS, AFTER ALL...

...AND HOLLOWED-OUT PUMPKINS?

THEY'RE EASY TO **SMASH!**

KLURPSH

THE KEY IS COMMITMENT! HIT 'EM WITH EVERYTHING YOU'VE GOT!

KEEP YOURSELF CLEAR OF THEIR MOUTHS, THOUGH!

THPLOCKK

THIS WOULD BE A LOT EASIER IF WE HAD SOMETHING TO HIT THEM WITH!

SNAP

CAROL!

KRCH

THERE'S NO WAY WE CAN KEEP THIS UP. THERE ARE HUNDREDS OF THEM!

THEN WE SMOOSH AS MANY AS WE CAN. EACH PUMPKIN THAT'S CAVED IN IS ONE THAT'S NOT GOING TO EAT SOMEONE.

THERE'S BITTERWOOD!

LOTS OF PUMPKINS AFTER HER!

SHE **IS** A JERK. MAYBE THE PUMPKINS LIKE THE TASTE OF JERKS BEST.

THEY **DID** POUNCE ON DEPUTY FINN PRETTY QUICK.

CAROL! NO SPEAKING ILL OF THE DEVOURED.

WE NEED TO HELP HER.

WE NEED TO HELP **EVERYONE!**

EVEN IF SHE DOESN'T KNOW ANOTHER WAY TO **STOP** THE PUMPKINS, SHE CAN TELL US HOW SHE MADE THEM COME TO LIFE!

AND THAT MIGHT GIVE US A CLUE FOR HOW TO STOP THEM ANOTHER WAY!

WHY DON'T WE STEP INSIDE?

EVERY PUMPKIN THAT CAUGHT SIGHT OF YOU DROPPED WHATEVER IT WAS DOING TO CHASE YOU. THEY SEE YOU AS A THREAT. WE'LL TRY TO PROTECT YOU...

...**YOU** TELL **US** HOW YOU MADE THE PUMPKINS COME TO LIFE.

I DIDN'T.

THE PUMPKIN PATCH IS **CURSED.**

IT HAS BEEN FOR MORE THAN **TWO HUNDRED YEARS.**

THE PATCH BELONGED TO MY ANCESTOR, DORCAS BITTERWOOD.

SHE WAS ENGAGED TO MARRY OBADIAH PUMPKINS—

THE OBADIAH PUMPKINS? FOUNDER OF PUMPKINS COUNTY?

THE VERY SAME. THEY BUILT A HOUSE ON DORCAS'S LAND, WHERE THEY INTENDED TO MOVE, AND DORCAS PLANTED PUMPKINS ALL AROUND IT.

SHE THOUGHT IT WOULD BE FITTING FOR **PUMPKINS** TO GROW AT THE **PUMPKINS** PLACE.

OBADIAH WAS OVERJOYED, AND HOSTED THE FIRST CARVING CONTEST AS PART OF THEIR WEDDING DAY, A DAY THAT WOULD BE THE COUNTY'S VERY FIRST FALL FESTIVAL.

BUT DURING THE CELEBRATION, OBADIAH WAS OFFERED A GREAT DEAL OF MONEY FOR THE HOUSE AND THE LAND. HE ACCEPTED.

DORCAS WAS INCENSED. THEY HAD BUILT THAT HOUSE TOGETHER. THEIR SWEAT, BLOOD, TEARS, AND LAUGHTER HAD SANCTIFIED THE EARTH ON WHICH IT STOOD AS A SYMBOL OF THEIR UNION.

THEY FOUGHT, AND OBADIAH STORMED AWAY, REFUSING TO SHARE A HOME WITH SUCH A STUBBORN WOMAN.

DORCAS HAD HER LAND, BUT SHE WAS HEARTBROKEN.

SHE WAS ALSO A **WITCH.**

SHE PLACED A CURSE ON THE LAND. PUMPKINS COUNTY WOULD NEVER AGAIN YIELD A CROP OF PUMPKINS, **EXCEPT** FROM THE PATCH THAT THEY HAD JOINTLY TENDED.

IT WOULD **FOREVER** GROW PUMPKINS, BUT THEY COULD **NEVER** BE TURNED INTO THE CHARMING JACK-O'-LANTERNS OF WHICH OBADIAH WAS SO FOND...

...NOT WITHOUT **TERRIBLE** CONSEQUENCES.

THE CURSE COULD BE LIFTED SIMPLY ENOUGH... OBADIAH NEEDED ONLY TO RETURN HOME AND GIVE HER A **KISS,** A GESTURE OF APOLOGY AND OF HIS INCLINATION TO REKINDLE THE LOVE THEY ONCE SHARED.

BUT OBADIAH WAS NO LESS STUBBORN THAN HIS ERSTWHILE BRIDE.

THEY NEVER SPOKE AGAIN, AND SO THE CURSE REMAINS TO THIS DAY.

IT WAS A BLOOD CURSE, WHICH MEANS IT CARRIES TO DESCENDANTS. I'M PROBABLY THE LAST OF THE BITTERWOODS, SO THE CURSE MAY DIE WITH ME. BUT I MIGHT HAVE A DISTANT COUSIN OUT THERE, SO DON'T FIGURE ON PUTTING ME IN THE GROUND TO STOP THE PUMPKINS, THANK YOU.

IF THE CURSE CARRIES TO RELATIVES, COULDN'T YOU BREAK IT?

BY KISSING AN ANCESTOR OF OBADIAH? SORRY, KID. THERE HASN'T BEEN ANYONE IN PUMPKINS COUNTY WITH THE LAST NAME **PUMPKINS** SINCE BEFORE I WAS BORN.

WE'RE STUCK WITH THIS CUR—

CRASH

GET IN!

I'D RATHER BE EATEN ALIVE THAN SHARE A TRUCK WITH *YOU*, OBIE KRAUT!

COME ON!

HURRY, HURRY!

VROOOOOM

WELL, SAMANTHA, YOU SURE PLAYED **ME** FOR A FOOL.

HA!

YOU DON'T NEED ANY HELP FROM ME IN THAT DEPARTMENT.

WHERE ARE YOU TAKING US?

PUMPKINS THAT **WERE** CHASING OTHER FOLK TURNED WHEN THEY SAW **YOU** COME OUT AND STARTED MAKING TOWARD YOU. I RECKON THEY'RE DRAWN TO YOU.

SO WE'RE GOING TO LEAD THIS LITTLE ARMY OF YOURS **AWAY** FROM THE PEOPLE THEY'RE CURRENTLY TRYING TO **EAT.**

PUMPKINS CO

SHERIFF'S DEPT

GUESS THIS'LL TEACH ME TO THINK I KNOW A PERSON.

FOR THIRTY YEARS I'VE DEFENDED YOU AGAINST EVERY SORT OF RUMOR.

WELL, I SURE AS SPITFIRE DIDN'T ASK YOU TO.

SHERIFF! PULL ACROSS THE COURTHOUSE LAWN.

I'D BETTER HAVE A GOOD REASON FOR DOING THIS, JARVIS!

KEEP 'ER STEADY, SHERIFF!

YOINK!

A PUMPKIN?!

IN CASE YOU HAVEN'T NOTICED, KIDS, WE'RE TRYING TO GET **AWAY** FROM THE PUMPKINS!

THIS ISN'T JUST **ANY** PUMPKIN, SHERIFF OBIE...

...THIS BABY'S GOT **FLASH!**

"FLASH"?

JARVIS, WHAT DID YOU DO TO YOUR PUMPKIN?

I WANTED IT TO BE **EXTRA-SPECIAL** FOR THE CONTEST, SO I OPENED IT UP, SCOOPED IT CLEAN, AND LINED THE INSIDE WITH A LITTLE COMPOUND I COOKED UP...

...SOME SUGAR, POTASSIUM CHLORATE, A LITTLE BIT OF BAKING SODA, AND SOME GREEN WAX TO GIVE IT THAT JARVIS CLARK TOUCH.

SINCE YOU CAN'T BRING A PUMPKIN THAT'S ALREADY BEEN SCOOPED TO THE CONTEST, I SEALED MINE BACK UP WITH A MELTED ORANGE CRAYON SO NO ONE COULD TELL.

JARVIS! THAT'S CHEATING!

I DON'T CARE ABOUT **WINNING.** I JUST WANTED MY PUMPKIN TO BE THE MOST MEMORABLE. IT'S NOT CHEATING IF YOU DON'T CARE ABOUT WINNING.

IT IS SO STILL CHEATING!

SHERIFF, THE ATTACK-O-LANTERNS ARE CLOSING IN!

AND THERE'S A WHOLE LOT OF THEM!

95

DO ANY OF **YOU** GUYS HAVE A LIGHTER?

I'VE GOT THE NEXT BEST THING.

PUMPKINS CO

SHERIFF'S DEPT.

GOTCHA!

THE TOP! TAKE OFF THE TOP!

SNAP SNAP

THE TOP?

TO GET THE CANDLE OUT!

GOOD RIDDANCE!

HERE YOU GO, JARVIS!

LIGHT THE INSIDE OF MY PUMPKIN!

THERE'S NO CANDLE!

JUST TOUCH IT TO THE INSIDE.

THE CHLORATE WILL IGNITE...

BUT THE SODIUM BICARBONATE — BAKING SODA — WILL KEEP IT FROM ALL GOING UP AT ONCE.

SO WHAT YOU'VE GOT...

...IS A GRADE-A **SMOKE-BLOWER!**

I'M NOT STOPPING FOR JARVIS. I WANT TO MAKE SURE THAT WE DON'T GET TOO FAR AHEAD OF THOSE PUMPKINS.

ARE YOU KIDDING? THERE ARE HUNDREDS OF THEM GANGING UP ON US! WE NEED TO GET AS FAR AHEAD AS WE CAN!

IF THEY LOSE SIGHT OF US, THEY MIGHT LOSE INTEREST. AS LONG AS THEY'RE CHASING **US**, THEY'RE NOT **EATING** PEOPLE. SO WE LET THEM CATCH UP AGAIN.

AT LEAST THERE'S SOME **JUSTICE** IN THIS WHOLE THING.

JUSTICE?

HE MEANS HE'S GLAD THAT THOSE PUMPKINS SEEM KEEN ON EATING **ME.**

I WOULDN'T WISH DEATH-BY-PUMPKIN ON NOBODY, BUT IF ANYONE DESERVES IT, I RECKON IT'S THE PERSON WHO PUT THEM ON THIS MURDEROUS PATH.

YOU'RE AS FAIR-MINDED AS A RABID SLUG, OBIE KRAUT.

I CAN'T BELIEVE I WAS GONNA MARRY YOU.

MAYBE WE DON'T HAVE TO!

SHERIFF OBIE, YOU SAID OBADIAH IS A FAMILY NAME...

...IS THERE ANY CHANCE YOU'RE DESCENDED FROM OBADIAH PUMPKINS, THE COUNTY'S FOUNDER?

MORE THAN A CHANCE. HE WAS MY GREAT-GREAT-GREAT-GREAT GRANDPAPPY.

WHAT? YOU NEVER TOLD ME THAT!

I'M A HUMBLE MAN, SAMANTHA.

BRAGGING ABOUT BEING **PUMPKINS COUNTY ROYALTY** AIN'T MY STYLE.

SHERIFF, **YOU'VE** GOT THE POWER TO STOP THESE PUMPKINS!

OH, NO! I AM **NOT** KISSING **THAT** OLD BADGER.

KISSING? WHY IN THE FILTHY BLUE MOON WOULD I KISS **YOU?**

BECAUSE IT'LL BREAK THE CURSE!

WHAT CURSE?

SMASH

THAT ONE NEARLY HAD US!

ANCIENT CURSE! PUMPKIN REVENGE! NO TIME FOR DETAILS, BUT **YOU** AND YOU **ALONE** CAN BREAK THE CURSE WITH A KISS!

AND I'VE GOT TO KISS **HER?**

KISSING ME IS A PRIVILEGE AWARDED TO **VERY** FEW, OBIE KRAUT, SO WATCH YOUR TONE!

I GUESS IF IT'LL SAVE THE COUNTY, I **COULD** CHOKE DOWN MY VOMIT AND PLANT A SMOOCH ON HER LEATHERY OLD LIPS.

...BUT OUR PURSUERS CAN'T!

AUGH!

IT'S LIKE A PUMPKIN-PARTS METEOR SHOWER!

DID THEY ALL SMASH?

I DON'T THINK THERE ARE ENOUGH OF THEM LEFT TO FORM UP AS A GIANT PUMPKIN MONSTER AGAIN, BUT THERE ARE STILL PLENTY ROLLING AND HOPPING AFTER US!

NOW THAT THEY CAN'T TAKE CITY-BLOCK STRIDES, WE OUGHT TO BE ABLE TO STAY AHEAD.

NO SUCH LUCK.

LOOKS LIKE WE RUPTURED THE GAS TANK BOUNCING DOWN THAT HILL OR TEARING THROUGH THE CORN FIELD.

OUR FUEL IS LEAKING FAST! DOUBT WE'VE GOT A HALF MILE'S WORTH LEFT.

110

TURN LEFT!

THAT HEADS US BACK TOWARD DOWNTOWN!

IT'LL BRING US PAST THE BITTERWOOD PATCH! DOC, ARE YOU SURE THERE'S NOTHING WITCHY THERE WE CAN USE TO STOP THE ATTACK-O-LANTERNS?

NOT A DANG THING...

...BUT IF I'VE GOT TO MEET MY END, I GUESS HOME IS AS GOOD A PLACE TO GET EATEN AS ANYWHERE ELSE.

HECK, MAYBE WE CAN HOLE UP AND BUY OURSELVES A FEW EXTRA MINUTES OF BREATHING BEFORE THEY TAKE US OUT.

SAMANTHA BITTERWOOD! ARE YOU INVITING ME IN?

DON'T MAKE A PARADE OUT OF IT, OBIE KRAUT.

D'YOU KNOW WE DATED NEAR TWO YEARS AND I NEVER SAW THE INSIDE OF HER HOUSE?

HECK, YESTERDAY WAS THE FIRST TIME I EVEN SET FOOT INSIDE HER DADGUMMED FENCE!

THAT'S IT FOR OUR FUEL.

VRMM PUTPUTPUTPUTPUT phut!

WELL, NOW YOU KNOW THE REASON FOR IT. THAT PATCH WAS CURSED, OBIE.

I COULDN'T RISK ANYONE BEING AROUND IT, GETTING TEMPTED TO TAKE A PUMPKIN. YOU SAW WHAT HAPPENS!

YOU MEAN YOU DIDN'T BRING THESE THINGS TO LIFE IN THE FIRST PLACE?

OBIE, MY WHOLE LOUSY LIFE HAS REVOLVED AROUND TRYING TO **PREVENT** IT!

I HAD TO BE ON HAND ANYTIME THE PUMPKINS WERE ON THE VINE, TO MAKE SURE THAT NO ONE CAME AND TOOK ONE.

ONE — JUST ONE — GOT TAKEN FROM THE PATCH BACK WHEN MY GREAT-GRANDMOTHER TENDED IT. IT ATE A WHOLE FAMILY.

I WAS TOLD THAT STORY FROM THE TIME I WAS YOUNG. MY MOTHER WANTED ME TO UNDERSTAND THE RESPONSIBILITY ON MY SHOULDERS.

IF I WANTED TO PROTECT PEOPLE FROM THE CURSE, I COULD **NEVER LEAVE.** HECK, THE FARTHEST I'VE EVER GONE IS ACROSS THE RIVER TO BASKERVILLE.

WITH THE VINES BARE IN THE SPRING I COULD TAKE CLASSES THERE. I COULDN'T BREAK THE CURSE, BUT I THOUGHT THAT IF I STUDIED PLANTS, I MIGHT LEARN A WAY TO KEEP THE PUMPKINS FROM GROWING YEAR AFTER YEAR.

NO LUCK. I'VE POISONED THEM, DUG UP THE ROOTS, SALTED THE EARTH, AND A DOZEN OTHER THINGS. THEIR MAGIC IS TOO POWERFUL. SO I'VE BEEN STUCK HERE, TRYING TO PROTECT EVERYONE.

THAT'S WHY YOU WOULDN'T COME WITH ME WHEN I WENT OFF TO STUDY LAW ENFORCEMENT?

CAN'T THINK OF ANOTHER REASON, EXCEPT THAT YOU TURNED OUT LOOKING LIKE A THUMB WITH A MUSTACHE.

THEY'RE COMING!

I ALWAYS THOUGHT YOU JUST COULDN'T UNDERSTAND HOW I FELT, COMPELLED TO DEDICATE MY LIFE TOWARD KEEPING PEOPLE SAFE...

...BUT I GUESS ME AND YOU AREN'T SO DIFFERENT AFTER ALL.

WHY DIDN'T YOU JUST TELL ME ABOUT THE CURSE?

I DIDN'T THINK YOU'D WANT TO BE WITH ME IF YOU KNEW I CAME FROM A LONG LINE OF **WITCHES.**

SAMANTHA, YOU COULD'VE BEEN LIME GREEN AND COVERED HEAD TO TOE WITH WARTS, AND THAT WOULDN'T HAVE KEPT ME FROM LOVING YOU.

HEY!

THERE ARE SOME GARDENING TOOLS OVER HERE!

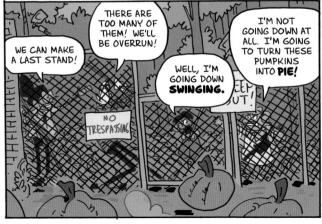

THERE ARE TOO MANY OF THEM! WE'LL BE OVERRUN!

WE CAN MAKE A LAST STAND!

WELL, I'M GOING DOWN **SWINGING.**

I'M NOT GOING DOWN AT ALL. I'M GOING TO TURN THESE PUMPKINS INTO **PIE!**

NO TRESPASSING

THEY DON'T HAVE ANY INSIDES ANYMORE! THAT'S WHAT YOU USE TO MAKE PIE.

JUST LET ME PSYCH MYSELF UP FOR BATTLE, JARVIS!

SHERIFF, YOU WANT A SHOVEL OR A PITCHFORK?

NEITHER.

WHEN THAT WAVE OF PUMPKINS HITS US...

...I'D RATHER BE HOLDING **SAMANTHA** THAN A **SHOVEL.**

DADGUMMIT, OBIE KRAUT, IT'S TAKEN ME THIRTY YEARS TO NURSE THIS GRUDGE ON YOU.

DON'T YOU UNDO ALL MY HARD WORK WITH YOUR ROMANTIC NOTIONS!

GREAT. MY LAST MOMENTS IN THIS WORLD ARE SPENT AS A SUPPORTING PLAYER IN A TRAGIC OLD-PEOPLE LOVE STORY.

THEY'RE CRESTING THE WALL!

115

UNGH... IS EVERYONE OKAY?

I JUST HAD ABOUT A HUNDRED PUMPKINS LAND ON ME, SO IT'S TOUGH TO SAY.

AT LEAST THEY WERE HOLLOW. OTHERWISE, WE'D BE SMOOSHED FLAT!

WHAT STOPPED THEM? WAS IT BEING IN THE PUMPKIN PATCH?

I DIDN'T **BELIEVE** THE STORIES MY MOTHER TOLD ME WHEN I WAS A GIRL.

I THOUGHT SHE WAS JUST SPINNING YARNS TO KEEP ME FROM LEAVING HOME.

SO ONE DAY I SNUCK OUT AND MADE A JACK-O'-LANTERN OF MY OWN TO SEE IF HER WARNINGS WERE TRUE.

DID IT TRY TO EAT YOU?

I CARVED **MY** LITTLE MONSTER RIGHT HERE IN THIS PATCH, AND THE CURSE WAS JUST AS ACTIVE HERE AS ANYWHERE ELSE.

IT WASN'T COMING HOME THAT STOPPED THOSE PUMPKINS. IF I DIDN'T KNOW BETTER, I'D SAY IT WAS THAT KISS.

BY THE WAY, THAT WAS A CORKER OF A KISS THERE, OBIE. NICE JOB.

BUT I **DO** KNOW BETTER.

118

ME AND SAMANTHA BROKE THE CURSE. WITH OUR SMOOCHIN'!

YEAH!

BUT IF WE HADN'T SAVED HER FROM THE PUMPKINS FIRST—

YOU MEAN AFTER YOU PIPED AWAY THE POTION THAT WOULD'VE KEPT THEM FROM COMING TO LIFE IN THE FIRST PLACE?

OH. YEAH.

WELL, WE FIGURED OUT HOW TO PERMANENTLY BREAK THE CURSE, SO AT LEAST NO ONE IS IN DANGER FROM YOUR PATCH ANYMORE!

THAT'S TRUE. AND IT'S THE ONLY REASON I DON'T TURN THE LOT OF YOU INTO TOADS!

NOW, SAMANTHA, LET'S CUT THEM A LITTLE SLACK.

IT'S NOT ENTIRELY THEIR FAULT THAT THEY'RE ALWAYS GETTING INTO TROUBLE.

THEY JUST AREN'T BEING KEPT BUSY ENOUGH.

BUT DON'T WORRY. I'VE STILL GOT THEM FOR SERVICE DETENTION...

ABOUT THE AUTHOR

Chris Schweizer has never seen a ghost, but he's worked in three places that were supposed to be haunted: an old restaurant, an old mental hospital, and an old hotel. When he was in college, he lived in a house that *The Week* magazine later called "The Most Haunted Place in England."

Chris has been a college professor, a hotel manager, a movie theater projectionist, a guard at a mental hospital, a martial arts instructor, a set builder, a church music leader, a process server, a life-drawing model, a bartender, a car wash attendant, a bagboy, a delivery boy, a choirboy, a lawn boy, a sixth-grade social studies teacher, a janitor, a speakeasy proprietor, a video store clerk, a field hand, a deckhand, a puppeteer for a children's television show, a muralist, a kickboxer, and a line worker at a pancake mix factory. He likes being a cartoonist best. He lives in Kentucky with his wife and daughter.

COLLECT THEM ALL!